My
DOUBLE-EDGED
LIFE

ZONDERVAN

My Double-Edged Life
Copyright © 2008 by Funnypages Productions, LLC

Requests for information should be addressed to:
Zondervan, Grand Rapids, Michigan 49530

Library of Congress Cataloging-in-Publication Data
Krueger, Jim.
My double-edged life / written by Jim Krueger ; illustrated by Ariel Padilla ; created by
Tom Bancroft and Rob Corley.
   p. cm. -- (Tomo ; v. 2)
"Published in association with Funnypages Productions, LLC."
ISBN-13: 978-0-310-71301-2 (pbk.)
1. Graphic novels. I. Padilla, Ariel, 1968- II. Bancroft, Tom. III. Corley, Rob. IV. Title.
PN6727.K74M9 2007
741.5'973--dc22
                            2007005081

This book published in conjunction with Funnypages Productions, LLC, 106 Mission
Court, Suite 704, Franklin, TN 37067

Series Editor: Bud Rogers
Managing Editor: Bruce Nuffer
Managing Art Director: Merit Alderink

My Double-Edged Life

SERIES EDITOR
BUD ROGERS

STORY BY
JIM KRUEGER

ART BY
ARIEL PADILLA

funnypages
PRODUCTIONS

ZONDERVAN®

ZONDERVAN.com/
AUTHORTRACKER
follow your favorite authors

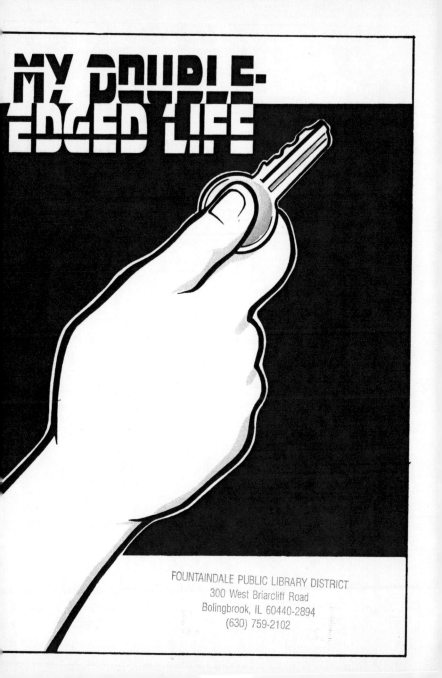

MY DOUBLE-EDGED LIFE

"HE WOULD GIVE
THE SWORD TO
ARDATH."

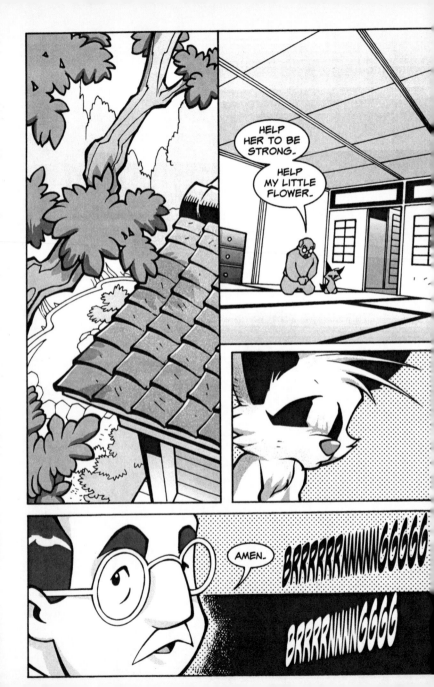

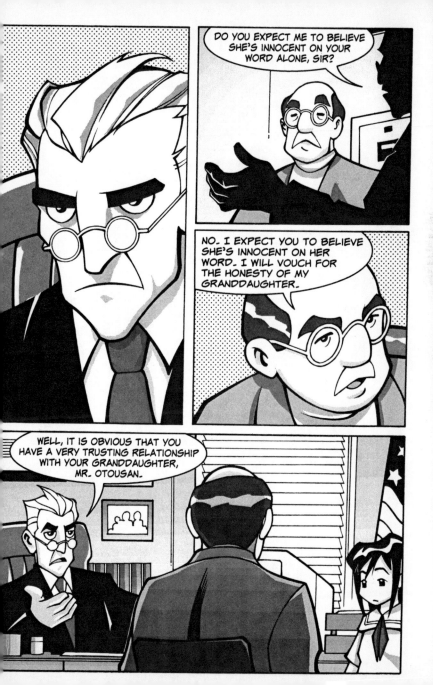

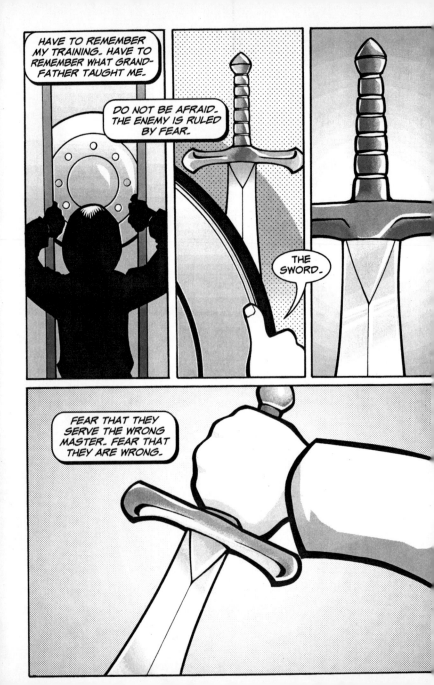

ZONDERVAN®

We want to hear from you. Please send your comments
about this book to us in care of zreview@zondervan.com. Thank you.

Grand Rapids, MI 49530
www.zonderkidz.com

ZONDERVAN.com/
AUTHORTRACKER
follow your favorite authors